W9-AWF-837

Stories from the Big Chair

Also by Ruth Wallace-Brodeur

Stories from the Big Chair

Ruth Wallace-Brodeur
illustrated by Diane de Groat

Margaret K. McElderry Books
NEW YORK

To Anne Georgia
R W-B

A special thank-you to my models
Anne and Katharine
DdG

Margaret K. McElderry Books
Macmillan Publishing Company
866 Third Avenue
New York, NY 10022
Collier Macmillan Canada, Inc.

Printed in the United States of America
First Edition
10 9 8 7 6 5 4 3 2 1

Library of Congress Cataloging-in-Publication Data
Wallace-Brodeur, Ruth.
Stories from the big chair / Ruth Wallace-Brodeur. — 1st ed.
p.   cm.
Summary: Molly tells her parents seven stories about herself and
her younger sister, recounting one story for each day of the week.
[1. Sisters—Fiction.   2. Family life—Fiction.   3. Storytelling—
Fiction.]   I. de Groat, Diane, ill.   II. Title.
PZ7.W15883Su   1989   [E]—dc19   88-35230 CIP   AC
ISBN 0-689-50481-0

CONTENTS

MONDAY

"I am tired of having a sister," said Molly.

"Why?" asked Mama.

"Because she is always here," Molly said. "She is here at breakfast, lunch,

1

and supper. She is here all day and all night. I am tired of Susan. I wish I was an only child."

"Yes," said Mama. "That might be nice."

"Are you tired of Susan too?" Molly asked.

"No," Mama said. "Not right now."

"Well, I am," said Molly. "I am tired of Susan right now. I have been tired of her all day."

"Hmm." Mama was thinking. "Sometimes it helps to tell a story," she said.

"What story?" asked Molly.

"Your story," Mama said. "Molly's story."

"I don't have one," said Molly.

"Yes you do," Mama said. "You have lots of stories."

"Like what?" Molly asked.

"Well, let me see. Who puts the pancakes under the bird feeder for the squirrels?"

"I do," said Molly.

"And who wears her swim mask in the bathtub?"

"I do," said Molly.

"And who likes purple jam and purple ice cream and a purple hat?"

"I do," said Molly.

"Those are Molly stories," Mama said. "You have lots of Molly stories."

"Who do I tell them to?" Molly asked.

"I like stories," Mama said. "You can tell them to me."

"Okay," Molly said. "After supper we will sit in the big chair and I will tell you a story."

After supper, Molly and Mama sat

in the big chair. Molly wore her purple hat.

"Are you ready?" she asked Mama.

"Yes," Mama said. "I am ready."

So Molly began.

Once upon a time there was a girl named Molly. She lived at 44 Summer Street. She had brown hair and brown eyes. She had a scar on her knee from when she fell off the swing. She had a hole in her mouth where a tooth came out.

Molly had a friend named Mike. Mike's tooth came out, too. Molly could see the top of a new tooth in the hole where Mike's old tooth used to be. She couldn't see a new tooth in her hole.

"What if a new tooth doesn't grow in?" Molly asked.

4

"It will grow in," Mama said.

"Are you sure?" Molly asked.

"Yes," Daddy said. "It will grow in."

"What if it doesn't?" Molly asked.

"Then you will look funny," said Susan. Susan is Molly's sister. She is four years old. She has red hair.

Susan always does what Molly does. She is a copycat. If Molly goes out, Susan goes out. If Molly sings a song, Susan sings a song. If Molly plays with Paw, Susan plays with Paw. Paw is their cat.

After Molly's tooth came out, Susan tried to get her tooth out, too. She wiggled it. She pulled on it. She chewed some of Molly's bubble gum. Molly was chewing bubble gum when her tooth came out.

"Don't wiggle your tooth, Susan,"

Mama said. "It isn't time for it to come out yet."

"Don't pull on your tooth, Susan," Daddy said. "It isn't ready."

"Give me back my gum," Molly said.

"I want my tooth to come out," Susan said. "I want to put it under my pillow and get money, just like Molly."

"Do you want a hole in your mouth?" Molly asked. "Do you want to look funny like me, Susan?"

Susan was quiet. Then she said, "Don't worry, Molly. Your tooth will grow in. It isn't time yet. Your tooth will grow in when it's ready."

"That's the end of the story," said Molly. "And guess what? I can see the top of my new tooth."

Mama looked in Molly's mouth. "Yes," she said. "There it is."

"Sometimes Susan is nice," Molly said. "Even if she is a copycat."

TUESDAY

"I am still a little tired of Susan,"
Molly said.

"You are?" said Mama.

"Yes," said Molly. "Maybe I need to
tell another story."

"Okay," Mama said. "I'll meet you
in the big chair after supper."

9

"Are you ready?" asked Molly when she and Mama were sitting in the big chair.

"Yes," said Mama. "I'm ready."

So Molly began.

Once upon a time, there was a girl named Molly. Molly went to school. Her sister, Susan, didn't. Susan was too little. Molly went to school with her friend Mike.

"Do you want me to go with you?" Mama asked on the first day of school.

"No," Molly said. "You came when I was in first grade. This year I will go with Mike."

Molly sat on the steps to wait for Mike. When Mike came, he showed Molly his lunch. He had a tuna fish sandwich, an apple, and three cookies.

"Paw loves tuna fish," said Molly. "Will you trade me a piece of your sandwich for some raisins?"

"Okay," Mike said. He gave Molly a little piece of his sandwich.

Molly gave him some raisins. Then she called Paw.

Mama and Daddy and Susan came out to say good-bye. Molly wanted to go to school, but she wasn't quite ready. "I think I forgot something," she said.

"What?" asked Daddy.

"Your lunch?" asked Mama.

"Tedda," said Susan. "You forgot Tedda." Tedda is Molly's bear. Susan ran and got her.

"That's silly," Mike said. "No one takes a bear to school."

"I would," said Susan. "I'd take my bear to school."

"You are little," Mike said. "Big kids don't take bears to school."

Molly gave her bear to Susan. "Put Tedda back on my bed," she said.

Molly kissed Mama and Daddy. She waved good-bye to Susan and Tedda. Paw walked with Molly and Mike to the end of the yard.

Molly felt sad all the way to the corner.

"Wait for me," she said to Mike. Molly ran back and got Tedda.

"People will laugh," Mike said. "No one takes a bear to school."

"I do," Molly said.

So did lots of kids. Six bears came to school on the first day.

"I wish I had my bear," said Mike.

"That's a good story," said Mama.

"Yes," said Molly. "I will tell you another one tomorrow."

WEDNESDAY

After supper, Molly put on her
purple hat. She got Tedda. Then she
sat in the big chair with Mama.

"Are you ready?" She asked Mama.

"Yes," said Mama. "I'm ready."

So Molly began.

Once upon a time, there was a girl named Molly. Molly loved jam. All kinds of jam.

"May I have some jam?" Molly asked Mama after school.

"You had jam and toast for breakfast," Mama said. "You had a jam and cheese sandwich for lunch. I think that is enough jam for today."

"She had jam for her snack, too," Susan said. "Molly took jam and crackers to school for her snack."

"I made some for you, Susan," Molly said. "You had jam too."

"If you are hungry, you may have an apple," Mama said.

"I don't want an apple," Molly said. "May I have just a little bit of jam?"

"No," said Mama. "You may have a carrot."

"I don't want a carrot," Molly said. "May I have just a tiny bit of jam?"

"No," said Mama. "You have had enough jam today. Don't ask again."

"Just a *teensy* bite?"

"Go to your room," Mama said.

Susan did not have to go to her room. Even though she had jam, too.

Pretty soon Susan came to the bedroom door. "Can I come in?" she asked.

"Go away," Molly said. "You told on me."

Susan went away. She came back with Paw. "Paw wants to play with you," she said.

"Paw can come in, but you can't," Molly said. Susan put Paw on

Molly's bed and went away.

Susan came back again. She had a paper bag. "Do you want to see what is in this bag?" she asked.

"No," Molly said.

"It's a present for you," said Susan. "A present you will like."

Molly played with Paw. She looked at a book. Susan was still there.

"Okay," Molly said. "What's in the bag?"

Susan opened the bag. She took out a jar of jam, a spoon, and some crackers. Molly put jam on a cracker and ate it. Then she fixed one for Susan. Susan sat on Molly's bed and they had some more.

Mama came to the door. "Supper is ready," she said.

Molly couldn't talk. Her mouth

was full. Susan had jam on her chin. Mama looked at them. She looked at the bag on the bed. "Come to supper," she said.

They had spaghetti and salad for supper. Mama and Daddy had ice cream for dessert. Susan and Molly had apples.

"I remember that," said Mama.

"Yes," said Molly. "You were there."

THURSDAY

After supper, Molly sat with Mama in the big chair.

"I'm glad you came," said Mama.

"Yes," said Molly. "I have another story. Are you ready?"

"I'm ready," Mama said.
So Molly began.

Once upon a time, there was a girl named Molly. Molly had a little sister named Susan. Everybody liked Susan.

They liked her red hair. They liked her because she was little. They liked her because she said funny things, and because she gave them hugs.

Mrs. Higgs likes Molly. She is Molly's friend. She lives on the same street. Molly can go to her house anytime. Susan can't. Daddy won't let Susan cross the street by herself.

Mrs. Higgs has brown eyes. She has white hair like a cloud. Sometimes Molly brushes Mrs. Higgs's hair while Mrs. Higgs reads to her. Then Mrs. Higgs says, "Now you

read to me, Molly. My eyes are tired." If Molly doesn't know a word, she makes one up. Mrs. Higgs likes the words Molly makes up.

Mrs. Higgs tells Molly about when she was a little girl. She had a sister, too. Her name was Lila. Lila had curly hair. "She looked like an angel," Mrs. Higgs said. "She could sing like one too."

Mrs. Higgs had a doll named Anna. "Anna was the only doll I ever liked," Mrs. Higgs said. "She had a china head, with blue eyes that opened and shut. She had silky brown hair and a soft body."

Lila liked Anna too. She had her own doll, but she liked Anna better. One day when Mrs. Higgs was at school, Lila took Anna outside. She left Anna on a stone wall. Anna fell

24

off and broke her head. She got all dirty.

"My father fixed her," Mrs. Higgs said. "But she was never the same."

Molly tells Mrs. Higgs stories, too. She tells her about school. She tells her about Susan.

Mrs. Higgs will always be Molly's friend. Even when Susan is big enough to cross the street.

"I like Mrs. Higgs," Mama said at the end of the story.

"Me too," said Molly.

FRIDAY

"Daddy says it's his turn to have a story," said Mama.

"Okay," said Molly. "After supper I will tell Daddy a story in the big chair."

"Once upon a time," Molly began, when she and Daddy were sitting in

the big chair, "there was a girl named Molly."

"I think I know her," Daddy said.

"Maybe," said Molly. "Now listen to the story."

Molly and her friend Mike had a club. It was for kids whose names begin with *M*. *Molly* begins with *M*. *Mike* begins with *M*. *Susan* does not begin with *M*. Susan is Molly's little sister.

Susan wanted to come to the club. Molly and Mike said "No."

"If you let me come, I will do what you tell me to do," Susan said.

Molly and Mike said no.

"I will not say a word," said Susan.

Molly and Mike said no.

"I will be it if we play hide and seek," said Susan.

Molly and Mike said no. "You are too little to be in our club," Molly said, "and your name does not begin with *M*."

"I hate you," Susan said. "You stink."

Susan went in the house. Molly and Mike went to find a place for the club. They looked at the end of the street. There are no houses at the end of the street. There is tall grass, some trees, and a big puddle after it rains. It's a good place for a club.

Molly and Mike sat under a tree. The tree was near the big puddle.

"We can make an *M* here with rocks," Molly said. They got some rocks and made an *M*. Then Molly pulled a hair from Mike's head and Mike pulled a hair from Molly's head. They put them under one of the rocks. Then they put their hands

on the rock and Molly said, "I will never tell where this club is." Mike said it, too. They threw some rocks in the puddle and made bark boats. Then they went home.

"Where is Susan?" Daddy asked.

"I don't know," Molly said.

"She isn't here," Daddy said.

Molly looked for Susan. Daddy looked for Susan. Molly went to Mike's house.

"Did you see Susan?" she asked. "We can't find her."

"I will help you look," said Mike.

They went to the end of the street. "I hear her," Molly said. "She's crying."

Susan was sitting in the mud by the puddle. Her shoe was stuck in the mud.

"Don't cry," Molly said. "We'll help you." Molly and Mike pulled

Susan and her shoe out of the mud. They took her home.

"Where were you?" Daddy asked.

"I was looking for Molly and Mike," Susan said. "I got stuck in the mud."

"You must not play at the end of the street," Daddy said. "You are too little."

"Sometimes the club will meet at our house," Molly said. "Then Susan can come too. Her name begins with *M* now. She is Muddy Susan."

"Is that the end of the story?" Daddy asked.

"Yes," said Molly.

"Susan is lucky," Daddy said.

"Why?" asked Molly.

"She has Molly for a sister," said Daddy.

SATURDAY

"Who will sit in the big chair with me tonight?" Molly asked.

"I will do Eeeny Meeny Miney Moe," said Susan.

> "Eeny meeny miney moe,
> Catch a rabbit by the toe,
> If he hollers let him go,
> Out goes Y-O-U!"

Susan pointed to Mama. "Daddy sits with Molly in the chair. Mama plays with me."

Molly got her purple hat. "Are you ready?" she asked Daddy.

"I'm ready," Daddy said.

So Molly began.

Once upon a time, there was a girl named Molly. She and her little sister, Susan, got their father a kite for his birthday. It was a dragon kite, with lots of colors and a long tail.

"I will wrap it," Susan said.

"We will both wrap it," Molly said. Susan put the paper on, and Molly tied the ribbon.

"I will hide it under my bed," Susan said.

"Paw will get it," Molly said. "Paw likes ribbons. Let's put it in the closet."

Susan got out of bed first on Daddy's birthday. She took the kite out of the closet. "Come on, Molly," she said as she ran out of the room. She didn't wait for Molly.

Daddy was still in bed. "Happy birthday!" Susan yelled. She gave him the kite. Daddy liked the kite, but Molly didn't like Susan.

After supper they had a birthday cake. Mama lit the candles. She turned out the lights.

"I will carry the cake," Susan said.

"It's my turn," Molly said. "You gave Daddy the kite. I will give him the cake."

"I want to carry the cake," Susan said. "It's my turn. You always carry the cake."

"No," Molly said. "You always get your way, Susan. I am going to carry the cake."

"I hope somebody does before my candles melt," Daddy said.

Susan stuck out her lip. She looked like she was going to cry and spoil the birthday party.

"Come and sit with me, Susan," Mama said. "Come and sing 'Happy Birthday' with me."

Susan sat on Mama's lap. "You can carry the cake this time, Molly," Susan said. "But next time it's my turn."

"Okay," Molly said.

Susan forgot that her own birthday is next.

Daddy laughed. "That's a good story," he said.

"Don't tell Susan," Molly said.

SUNDAY

Mama and Molly sat in the big
chair after supper. Paw sat on Mama's
lap. Tedda sat on Molly's.

"Are you ready?" Molly asked
Mama.

"Yes," Mama said. "I'm ready."

38

So Molly began.

Once upon a time, there was a girl named Molly. Molly sleeps in the same room with her little sister, Susan. Molly's bed is by the window. Susan's bed is next to the door.

Mama and Daddy read to Molly

39

and Susan at bedtime. They kiss them good-night, then they turn out the light and go downstairs.

Susan and Molly don't go right to sleep. Sometimes Molly teaches Susan a song from school. Sometimes Susan tells Molly a story. Susan makes up good stories. The one Molly likes best is about a tiny elf who lives in a nutshell and gets caught by a witch.

Sometimes Molly and Susan play make-believe. They pretend Molly is a pilot and Susan is an animal doctor. Molly flies Susan to sick animals all over the world. It is very dangerous, but they always get there and make the animals better. Everybody is very happy that the animals are better and that Molly and Susan are safe.

Then Molly and Susan go to sleep. Molly tucks her blanket around her ear and under her chin. Susan pulls her blanket up over her head. If Molly has a bad dream, she gets in Susan's bed. If Susan has a bad dream, she gets in Molly's bed. They always bring their bears. The bears are sisters, too.

Mama gave Molly a hug. "That makes one week of stories," she said. "Are you still tired of Susan?"

"No," Molly said. "Not right now. But I have more stories to tell."

"Good," said Mama. "I will sit with you in the big chair tomorrow night after supper."

"What if Daddy wants a story?" Molly asked.

"Then we will do Eeny Meeny Miney Moe," said Mama.

**NEW YORK MILLS
PUBLIC LIBRARY**

401 Main Street
New York Mills, N.Y. 13417

(315) 736-5391

MEMBER

MID-YORK LIBRARY SYSTEM
Utica, N.Y. 13502